PARANORMAL SEX COLLECTION VOLUME 2

EXPLICIT DIRTY EROTICA SHORT STORIES

BLAINE TELLER

plicit Press
Erotica Fiction

CHAPTER 1

FUCKING AT THE BLOODY MILK BAR

SHE WORE A WAIST-LENGTH LEOPARD-SKIN COAT, a pink tube skirt that doubled as a halter bra, black knit gloves with the fingertips cut off, big sparkly jewelry bangles, and hoop earrings.

I'm not the kind of girl who goes for gaudy chic. I'm not a lesbian either, but something about her made me follow when she said, "This way, Slut!"

Her big short blonde hair and the sexy hallow of her neckline and a dreamy voice told me she wasn't a guy in drag. She was all woman. I guessed she simply liked fingering cunt. Walking out to her blue corvette got my pussy all in the heat, as her ass pushed that tube dress up and down, slowly riding it up her trim thighs.

.   .   .

By the time we reached her tiny car, the luscious blonde's pink ass cheeks showed. My nose got a whiff of her musky pussy scent. My nipples felt as hard as two wooden pegs. I decided this one time I'd experiment with the female sex.

"Get in!"

She didn't open the door. I stood there like a hussy waiting for the man to be a gentleman. She just revved the engine, looked at the top of my black thigh-high stockings, and said. "Nice garter belt."

I wore a little black dress. A string of white pearls draped my neck. On my left wrist is a simple watch to contrast with the leopard bracelet. On my small feet, I wore brown Uggs. I huffed and raised my leg up. I stepped across the threshold into her corvette's blue leather seat. My naked pussy flashed the commanding blonde, as I straddled the door and sat down. I guess that's what she wanted, to see my naked, damp quim.

She boldly reached out and stroked my pierced clit barbell. "Nice."

I pulled back to the back of the seat. However, the sexual urge rushed from my clit to my breasts and brains before my mouth opened into a moan.

. . .

"That's my leopard, kitty," she purred as she gunned the engine again and we took off. I held on for dear life.

When we hit the highway, she drove like an eagle diving for prey in the open field. She shifted her legs back and forth. She threw the shift forward. My eyes focused on her red lipstick at first. Then I shifted my focus to her long spread legs because the background outside flew by too fast to see anything but a blur.

"Touch me!"

I shifted my gold-clutch purse between my legs. Reaching over with my left hand, I gracefully slid my hands over her thigh. My hand dipped down. My teal blue sparkling fingernails disappeared inside her wet gash.

She shrieked at the top of her lungs. "That's it Bitch. Touch my fuckslot! Push your hand deeper!"

We had the entire highway all to ourselves when a trucker came by and honked his horn. That's when I noticed the strangest thing. The big short blonde woman's teeth sprouted two nice length vampire teeth! The trucker driving next to us wore a black cape and had a widow's peak of black hair slicked on his forehead. He bit his wrists and motioned for me to do the same.

. . .

I was horrified. I'd never fucked a vampire before. Not to mention virtually fucked a vampire. My garter belts attracted the guy the most. He stuck out his tongue and if his tongue wasn't long as a rope, I'd say I was dreaming. The highway stretched out before us. It was dusk and not a soul was in sight.

"I'm Valaria!" She yelled over the wind, blowing her blonde hair back and my own black hair. "I'm a vampire." She pointed, "That's my husband. He wants to suck your bloody pussy."

I closed my legs. "How did he know I was on my period?" I said.

   "He could smell you. Don't worry; I'm on mine as well." She shrieked to her husband as the white truck drove closer and closer. I was scared he would crash into us and knock us off the road.

I took my hand out of Valaria's soggy pussy and sure enough on the tip of my index finger; a drop of blood coated my teal blue fingernail. I smiled and brought her scent of musky pussy and iron to my mouth and licked my fingers.

Her trucker boyfriend nodded.

I smiled back, spread my legs, and parted my pussy folds, slick and wet. I suddenly felt massively horny and wanted someone, anyone, to lick my cooze. I was randy out of my mind. The danger and the fact this vampire couple wanted me gave me goosebumps.

Her trucker boyfriend motioned ahead.

I saw a beat-up old green truck coming on Valeria's side of the road. She drove on the wrong side all this time. I never noticed! Valaria swung behind her husband like a bat snipping up an insect as the beat-up old green truck passed by us. The old white man in his white beard absolutely horrified at us hogging the road.

Valaria's trucker boyfriend spotted a wide-open field ahead and turned down the slight embankment. Valeria followed right on his rear wheels and suddenly sped up and cut the truck off. She motioned for me to get on the hood of her car. I was feeling crazy and wild as the two of them by now. I hiked up my little black dress. Her husband got down from the truck. He walked up to me and said, "I love women in garters on Halloween night." I lay on my elbows trembling. My cunt seeped as Valeria's husband lowered his head. He raised the inside of my kneecaps to his ears and he chowed down.

I felt wonderful. His tongue uncurled inside my cunt and folded flat and snaked up inside my swollen womb. Normally, about this time, I began to get cramps and had a couple of Pamprin pills in my purse for the occasion. But his tongue went up all in my girlie plumbing and sucked out the blood like a pro. His sucking tickled and aroused me at the same time. My nipples swelled up. Valeria was not to be denied either. She chomped down on my dusky brown nubs and sucked so hard she brought out breast milk! She leaned her head back, squirted the milk down her gullet, and smiled. Her husband rose from my messy slot. Blood ran down the sides of his mouth just like in those old black and white vampire films.

The two of them took turns sucking my cunt and nubs. They switched off. Valeria's rope-like tongue probed around my womb walls until I quivered and screamed out my orgasm. Her husband kept sucking my milking tits. She and he kept exchanging places, giving me new and different sensations until I fainted.

When I woke up, I was in a motel room, and a note on the divan read, "Thank you for the meal. Hope to see you again at the Bloody Milk Bar next month,

Valeria and Her Husband

CHAPTER 2

HIS FAVORITE VAMP

THE MOON WAS WANING in the autumn sky.

Scarlet had her panties hiked up under her skirt. After turning a key into a bulky doorknob, she walked past the front threshold of the mansion. Staring cautiously from corner to corner, she looked to see if Mark was there, waiting for her. She would have hated to think that she had come before him, but there was no reason for him to be out too late. Once Mark had his blood fixed, he was usually lounging in the living room.

Scarlet was beautiful, as are most female vampires. With her long dark tresses, naturally rosy cheeks on pale skin, and bright eyes that seemed to stare into a person's soul, Scarlet was quite the seductress. It had made her a good hunter, but she cared to keep such a power in the safe confines of her heart. She could have a harem, even a dungeon, filled with vampires and human playthings to occupy her time. Still, nothing really satisfied her as much as one person, the one that turned her into what she was now...

. . .

"Are you done feeding, dear?" a voice said as a strong hand brushed Scarlet's cheek from
    behind.

She knew exactly who it was before she even turned around. She looked and smiled pleasantly He didn't have to say much after that. With bloody lips, he leaned down to kiss her. Scarlet was already melting before she opened her lips, inviting Mark to dip his tongue in and flick around in her willing mouth.

The night had only begun. Mark was already picking her up in his arms. Telepathically, Mark closed the door behind them as he floated up the stairs. His strong hands had already pried the woman's top open, unveiling her breasts and licking her nipples. Scarlet was bending her head, moaning and rubbing between her legs. Mark was sniffing in the air, smelling how wet Scarlet had already become.

"I do hope that I did not disturb your hunger," Mark said politely. "No," Scarlet said calmly. "I have fed."
    A bed invited the lovers. With his hands against her thighs, Mark spread the woman's legs and promptly started to pull down her panties. He instantly started to eat her. Scarlet loved Mark's lack of shyness and bent her head back, moaning and rubbing her tits as she felt the man penetrate her with his long tongue. She was always surprised by how willing he was! There was nothing that made her get as

freaky as him. Her eyes stared up at the ceiling as she thought about how they had met, years ago in New Orleans. He had fucked her rotten all those 200 years or more ago, and he could still fuck her now.

And fuck her he would. After ten minutes of deep licking, he had already had them both stripped and his cock was out, erect and throbbing. With ease, he slipped into his lover's hole and started to pump, penetrating Scarlet with a pressing push. The woman's moans were turning into screams. Her hand was rubbing and digging on the man's back. She didn't know how to contain herself.

"God," Mark said to himself as he got more excited, pulling into the woman and popping into her hole with an intense push. She was always so firm, so wet, and gripped his dick with a loving touch.

"Fuck me," Scarlet demanded with intensity.

He loved meeting up to Scarlet's demands. There were things that he could do to her that no one could, which was why she had stayed with him for so long. Scarlet would always be his number one vampire.

"Oh, gods... fuck, just... give it to me!" Scarlet screamed as she felt the vampire dig into her hole like a stake, stabbing at her g-spot like a heart.

. . .

"Fuck," Mark said with a groan. It was all he could say. He was honestly caught up in the woman's pussy with an unyielding concentration, making sure she felt good. The stamina he had for her didn't wane easily- he had to fuck her, get into her body, and make her drip all over his covers. She was staining everything- her cries and her screams were completely filling the room. He could feel the heat vibrating from her womb, her breath feeling so nice and heavy against her skin. As their motions grew faster and faster, he could feel Scarlet pressing against him, meeting up with his rhythms, matching his pleasures.

Scarlet screamed so loudly.

"I'm going to fuck you until you cum," Mark said was heavy breaths. "I'm going to make you cum, vamp bitch."

"God," Scarlet said before screaming again.

"Hold on," Mark said as he reached his hands around to grasp Scarlet's. He wanted them to cum together. It was the thing that really made him feel like they were complete.

Their rhythms had gotten faster. Scarlet was moaning, biting the covers, and burying her head against the bed at points. She was no longer trying to keep her composure - at this point, they were animals, vampires in lust and love. She loved him more than she loved anyone she had ever known and would always be loyal to him. If only they could fuck like this forever.

As Mark shot his huge load into Scarlet, she felt herself orgasm as well. It was magical. The sweat and fire in their bodies brought them together, plastered by hot sex.

"God," Scarlet said. "I love you. I love you."

"And you," Mark said, sweating. "Now... we have much to do before the sun comes out."

CHAPTER 3

THE TASTE OF INNOCENCE: PART 2

ARTURO FLEW through midnight skies with his scarlet princess beside him as they swirled above the city like two passionate vapors in love with one another. Arturo was so in love with her and she was enchanted by his raw exotic beauty. Her eyes tell the tale of the gypsy queen who holds the secrets to the ways of the wisps of night. Her eyes have told the tale for centuries, of her who walks and sleeps with her lover Arturo in the cold dampness of the hidden cave. For centuries, they have made love within the total blackness that surrounds them by day. And then, when the moon is full and the stars sparkle endlessly in the black void, they emerge to glide across the shadows like two whispers in a dream.

They melted in the deepest midnight as one drinking the breath of the other and feeding upon each other's veins of hot seduction. As she sucked, she gained power from his blood and she became pale and beautiful in the wind of midnight to Arturo who craved her every thought. They are no strangers of the night; indeed, they have feasted many times together in the stillness of the dark. Their love was as timeless as was their thirst for blood. Together they had become the blood-red passion that taints the edges of the moon on those cold desperate nights when all is silent and yet screams with the terror of enchantment. It was upon their lips that souls died and their hearts became a passion. Their moans were more like animal growls as they felt the erotic fury mount within. They were a glance into fate and the last winking out of reality. They were captured in their love and thirst for blood and lust. They too were prisoners of the dark.

They feasted upon each other's hungry and sweetened flesh. Arturo drank from her most sensitive places as her wings of pink opened wide for him to drink of. She would surrender her flesh to him willingly. The mere touch of his needle-sharp fangs upon her neck made her juices flow like blood down a victim's neck. His bites were pure ecstasy. And when she felt his cold stiff cock buried deep within her secret cave, her snarl would echo through the blackness of their cave. It was a ritual she lived for, even more than feeding. She craved his raw animal lust and returned it three-fold. She showered him with her gushes of pure ecstasy from every fold upon her ivory flesh. Her lips opened like a flower to feed him his nectar. He latched onto her cold pussy and fed from her buds filled with endless rain.

Arturo adored his beautiful vampire princess; she was the hope of his every desire and darkest passion when he cried out with flashing fangs in the midnight. His essence was revealed upon her ivory neck that tasted of ripened blood-red berries. Her body writhed under his sharpened diamond fangs as they glistened in the golden moonlight. He brought her to endless orgasmic delight as he fed upon her flesh as if it was his heart's command. He would stiffen and his cock became a rigid sword when he tasted the first drop of her carnation-colored wings of rapture. Her core would invite him in with a bloodlust no mortal man could survive. His thrusts were like lightning, her embrace like that of forever. Their passion was a never-ending echo that danced upon their flesh. They never tasted each other's desire, they WERE that in itself.

Arturo only drew breath to feed and please his beautiful vampiress. He had searched for centuries to find her crying on the street that fateful evening. Now centuries later he was more in love and rapture with her than ever before. Her eyes told the tale she had died for those many centuries before. She was his elusive forever and he her darkest knight. There was an echo between them that shivered with their trembled passion and their endless love. And that trembling rippled through the night like an eerie wind.

Their love had and would stand the eternal test of time. They flew like two shadows upon the midnight wind the air wisped gently through her burgundy curls that glimmered with flecks of moon dust as he guided her to their love den after a night of feeding upon the dark streets and alleys of the city. Sometimes they chose to feed in the forest like two starving wolves ready for the first chilling and rapturous sip of blood.

Afterward, they would fall chilled and impassioned into their kiss of eternal rhapsody. He lived for her every enchantment. Her only purpose was to be the goddess of blood-red desire he had always fantasized about. He delighted in her milky flesh that tasted of ripened berries and his mouth never tired of sinking deep within the furry jungle that lie between her icy thighs. His pendulant promise lay swollen and tinged blood red under his silk cape was demanding to be set free from its throbbing and rigid gloom.

He hungered for his dagger to ease into the depths of her velvet sheath. Once inside her dark tunnel of pleasure, his frozen hard dick did the dance of love in and out of his rhapsodic vampire. There was no breath of air but for the stars pleading in repose. She tasted of enchantment and smelled of devotion's will. There was no surrender, but yet yielded eagerness to be taken within the shadows He felt the rising at her command and pulled her tightly into his arms. The centuries had forgotten what their hearts would never leave behind. There was tenderness within their lust that immersed them in a pool of tepid red. They were not of the night but within the night and the wind held them gentle within her elusive embrace. The dark ones would remember what their prey would soon forget. There would be no end to their love or to the endless moonbeams that they rode. Alone as one they were the passion of a million. Their kiss would awaken the dead.

CHAPTER 4

TASTE OF INNOCENCE

ARTURO WAS NOT LOOKING FORWARD to another lonely night flying from here to there in hopes of finding a decent feed to satisfy his vampire thirst and hunger. He was exquisitely beautiful and women vampires and humans flocked to him. He wished for one night that he didn't have the overwhelming desire to feed upon their blood and ravage their necks.

There were plenty of vampiresses who desired to be his soul mate, but Arturo had always wanted a human girl as his lover. Their innocence intrigued him and turned him on sexually more so that the bold and blatant female vampires he had come across. This is why Arturo had become some-what of a loner. He fed alone, flew alone and most nights slept alone. He saw beautiful girls that he would die to have one taste of but he had the willpower to whisk himself away before plunging his fangs deep within their jugulars.

Everyone assumed that vampires were savage beasts that only had a hunger for blood, but Arturo also was a passionate man with a hunger for romance and love. As Arturo took form as a shadowed wisp of vapor above the midnight sky in hopes of finding an unsuspecting animal to quench his thirst on, in the alley he saw a form of a young woman. As he flew lower, he could see her more clearly. She was breathtakingly beautiful in a very opposite way than a vampire looks. She had ivory freckled skin and long copper red hair. She was crying as if someone had hurt her deeply. Arturo was soft-hearted even as a creature of the night so he whisked down beside her to see what was wrong. She first looked up in complete shock and wonder, but the deep midnight blue in Arturo's eyes mesmerized her.

Arturo took her hand in his and she immediately noticed how icy cold his hand was yet it was seething hot as well. She seemed a bit frightened until Arturo draped his cape around her thin shoulders to warm her. She looked up in Arturo's deep blue eyes with her pale olive eyes and Arturo was breathless and intrigued by her innocent yet erotic beauty. The allure of her porcelain neck brought Arturo's passion to a head and he fantasized about the milky sweetness of it as he bit into her. But he didn't want to destroy this ethereal beauty so innocent yet so sultry.

Much to Arturo's surprise, she looked up to him and asked if he would like to drink of her neck. At the touch of Arturo's lips, her surrender was complete. She only felt his fangs for a brief moment until a warmth slipped through her body and awoke her sensual needs. It was as if his penetration was demanded elsewhere other than the suppleness of her neck. She swooned at the pleasure he drank and felt his arousal deepening.

She seemed to melt within his arms and be transformed to an erotic place full of color and passion that seemingly lifted her from her feet and sent her swirling through the night sky as in a vapor. He could feel it too. With all of the strength he had felt flow into his cold flesh through the centuries, there was something different this time. He felt her blood not only feeding his body but his mind as well.

The two of them feeding off of each other the substance of love and lust mingled into the essence of raw passion. His hands sought not to break her neck, but to caress her full breasts tipped with excitement and her hand slipped to his stiffened cock, now rigid with the flow of her blood coursing through the vein on top.

As the elixir of their combined blood made its way to her pussy, she felt her lips throbbing with their needs together. It's as if she could feel his desire as well as her own and it made her body stiff with erotic pleasure like nothing human. She shuddered when his cold fingers slipped between her legs and plunged deep inside her swollen throbbing pussy.

Her moan was of pleasure and surrender at the same time. Her mind swirled with every moment she was leaving behind. She gripped his hard cock and felt him suck even harder at her tender neck. It filled her hand as it filled her mind. This, she thought amid the eroticism was her dream.

As he sucked her neck causing her orgasm to only increase and never let up, she sucked his rigid vampire rod until it pulsated and turned a blood-red color. His cock tasted of the most elegant and sweet wine she had ever had the pleasure of lapping. She felt a change come to her body and she began to feed upon her lover's veins.

As she fed, she felt glistening fangs form and her skin turn so pale it was silvery and opalescent. She wanted to sink her teeth into his rigid dick and yet at the same time she wanted to feel it sink into her pulsating pussy. Arturo looked at his vampire princess as the final changes took place. Her red hair became a burgundy mane of red curls enveloping her porcelain skin and her golden eyes glowed as they stood out glistening in the midnight moon. Her fangs were sharp and emblazoned like white diamonds in the light of the moon.

Arturo took his black velvet cape and enveloped the two of them with it as they together as one disappeared into a wisp of sultry smoke. The dark sanctuary was filled with the raw and untouched smell of hunger and passion and walls lined with years of crystalline gem formations in every color of the rainbow. Their sleep was tantric and erotic as if in an opiated state until the owl sounded another evening at hand, as the two wrapped in Arturo's cape burst from their lair like lightening on yet another midnight feeding frenzy and another day to be impassioned with one another for centuries that would have no end.

CHAPTER 5

THE HAUNTED HOUSE

AN EROTIC TALE

THE LAST FEW weeks had been a tremulous one. Ever since Maya and her husband Luke moved into their new home, Luke had changed. They argued about almost everything. Luke was a few years older than Maya and was convinced that he was right, every time. Maya had always been a Christian woman, and she felt that the best thing to do was to visit her priest, Father Michael. It was then Father Michael explained the history of the old house on the hill where they now stayed. According to Father Michael, it was haunted. The family who lived there before her had been brutally murdered by a mad man, Thomas Cant, whose spirit was supposedly still in the house, haunting the souls of anyone who lived there. Maya invited him to visit the house to cast out any evil spirits that resided there.

That evening when her husband came home he seemed like a completely different man. "I'm sorry about all the fighting honey," he said.

Maya was momentarily taken in by his apology. Her

husband was not an apologetic man, even when he knew he was dead wrong.

He continued apologizing for his erratic behavior over the last few days, suddenly pulling her against his chest, crushing her mouth with a bruising kiss, sucking and biting her lips, his tongue forcing her mouth open. Maya didn't try to resist.

"Maya..." Luke breathed her name. "I don't want to fight; I want us to enjoy our time here. I want us to build a home here and raise our family. I don't know what came over me, I love you." With that, his mouth was everywhere, kissing her neck, her cheeks, and the tops of her breasts. He pulled the bodice of her dress aside, exposing one breast, covered by her lace bra. He tugged the cup of the bra down, her breast now exposed, forced up by the confines of the bra and dress.

Luke bent his head, capturing the nipple between his teeth, tugging it briefly before taking it into his mouth. He sucked on Maya's breast, hard, pulling the areola and the soft skin around it into his mouth.

Maya looked down at Luke's dark head, running her fingers through his curly hair as he suckled her. She felt a sharp tug deep within her, as she always did with Luke's rough sucking. She wanted to be mad at him, wanted to push him away but was powerless, and so she surrendered to the sensations swirling through her.

Luke continued working her breast with his mouth, his tongue swirling around her hard nipple. He worked his other hand beneath her dress, pulling her panties aside, running his fingers over her swollen pussy, Maya shuddering beneath his touch.

She ran her hand down his chest, reaching for his cock, but bumping into his hand. She looked down, surprised to find he'd unzipped his pants at some point and was stroking himself. She was confused; he'd never done that before.

Luke lifted his head from her breast, his eyes hot and heavy with passion. "Oh, babe, I've been so hot for you all afternoon. I kept thinking of you bent over my desk this morning. I was ready to burst." He smiled at her. "You can have full control of my cock now." He took her hand and guided it to his cock, folding her fingers around the shaft. "Touch me, Maya. Stroke my cock." His voice was low, seductive, but it was more of a command than a request.

He began thrusting his hips forward, his cock sliding in and out of her hand. "Oh, yeah...oh, babe, faster. That feels so good." Maya stroked his cock for a moment as he returned to kissing her deeply, roughly, his lips and tongue working her lips open, probing and claiming every recess of her mouth. His hands were mauling her breasts, tweaking her nipples, pulling and rubbing them between his fingers. He dropped his head to her neck with a moan, his breath hot against her skin.

Suddenly he was grunting against her, his hips twitching as his cock jumped in her hand, his whole body jerking. He pulled away from her with a ragged gasp, tearing his cock from her hand, turning her around with her back to him. He bent her over at the waist and pushed her dress up over her back.

"Oh, God! Maya...Oh, God." Luke's voice was almost panicked as he tried to get her in position. She felt his hands frantically pulling at her panties, pushing them aside, his cock poking against her ass as he worked to find an entrance to her pussy. He pushed her legs apart, spreading her ass with his hands as he did.

Suddenly, with one thrust, he pushed himself inside of

her, knocking her off balance, and making her cry out in surprise.

As she staggered forward, Luke grabbed her hips roughly, pulling her back. "Hold on, Maya," he rasped his voice rough. "Just hold still for a minute."

Luke began pounding into her hard, grunting with each thrust. *This is not making love*, thought Maya. *This is just fucking. What's going on here?*

Luke's rhythm quickly grew erratic, almost frantic, as he sought his release. He was gripping her hips tightly; Maya could feel his nails breaking the skin. She was almost unable to bear this pounding any longer, wanting to squirm away when he suddenly pulled her violently back against his cock. He made a sound she didn't recognize, something dark and primal, but vaguely familiar, as his orgasm finally broke. She could feel his massive cock explode inside of her, pumping out his hot load, filling her, and then running down her legs. He thrust several more times; fast, sharp strokes, as his cock pumped out the last of his load. He held himself inside her a moment longer, his cock still twitching, his hands clutching her hips.

When he finally pulled out of Maya, she stumbled forward, her legs and back cramping. Luke was breathing hard behind her, his hands on his knees, his body covered with sweat. She panicked; she thought he looked like he was having a heart attack.

"Are you okay?" She touched his shoulder. Luke stood a big self-satisfied smile on his face.

He pulled Maya to his chest.

"I'm fine, just catching my breath. That was amazing; you're amazing, Maya." He kissed her forehead. "This is just what I needed to get rid of the tension from today." He held her a moment longer and then took her hand, pulling her toward the bedroom.

As Maya looked into his eyes, she saw the man she knew, her husband. Not the crazed maniac who'd been physical with her, over the past few days. Yes, she knew then that her new house had been haunted but not anymore, thanks to Father Michael.

ABOUT THE AUTHOR

Blaine Teller is an emerging erotica author of many erotica kinks and sub-genres. Be sure to check out other books and leave a review if this story got you hot!

Visit my blog at Blaine Teller's Blog

Join my newsletter for the exclusive Blaine Teller's Newsletter

Sign up for Free Stories from Xplicit Press Authors

Xplicit Press Author Updates

Like Xplicit Press on Facebook

Follow Xplicit Press on Twitter

Readers: I want to expand a few of the stories to see where the characters can be explored further. If there are any of the stories that you would like to read more about again, I'd love to hear from you!

Keep In Touch
Blaine Teller
info@blaineteller.com